The Winnie-the-Pooh Winter Collection

of Stories and Poems

EGMONT

EGMONT

We bring stories to life

First published in Great Britain in 2015
by Egmont UK Limited,
The Yellow Building, 1 Nicholas Road, London W11 4AN
www.egmont.co.uk

Pooh Goes Hunting and *Piglet is Entirely Surrounded by Water* adapted from
Winnie-the-Pooh, first published 1926
Text by A.A.Milne copyright © Trustees of the Pooh Properties
Line illustrations copyright © E.H.Shepard
Colouring of the line illustrations copyright © 1970 and 1973
E.H.Shepard and Egmont UK Limited

A House is Built at Pooh Corner For Eeyore and *Piglet Does a Very Grand Thing* adapted from
The House at Pooh Corner, first published 1928
Text by A.A.Milne copyright © Trustees of the Pooh Properties
Line illustrations copyright © E.H.Shepard
Colouring of the line illustrations copyright © 1970 and 1974
E.H.Shepard and Egmont UK Limited

'Happiness' adapted from
When We Were Very Young, first published 1924
Text by A.A.Milne copyright © Trustees of the Pooh Properties
Line illustrations copyright © E.H.Shepard
Colouring of the line illustrations by Mark Burgess
copyright © 1989 Egmont UK Limited

'Us Two'; 'Waiting at the Window'; 'The Friend';
'The Engineer'; 'Sneezles'; 'Wind on the Hill';
'King John's Christmas' and 'In the Dark'
adapted from *Now We Are Six*, first published 1927
Text by A.A.Milne copyright © Trustees of the Pooh Properties
Line illustrations copyright © E.H.Shepard
Colouring of the line illustrations by Mark Burgess
copyright © 1989 Egmont UK Limited

ISBN 978 1 4052 7774 7
60176/1

Printed in China

The Winnie~the~Pooh Winter Collection

of Stories and Poems

A. A. Milne

with decorations by E. H. Shepard

Introduction

Winnie-the-Pooh was a stuffed bear belonging to A. A. Milne's son, Christopher Robin. He had started out in life as plain old Edward Bear, until Christopher re-named him; Winnie after a Canadian black bear he saw at London Zoo, and Pooh after the pet name given to a swan he fed every morning.

Winnie-the-Pooh came to the attention of the world on Christmas Eve 1925. This was the day a specially commissioned story appeared in a London newspaper, The *Evening News*. The story was called 'The Wrong Sort of Bees' and, after some re-working, became the first chapter in A. A. Milne's book *Winnie-the-Pooh*, published in 1926. A couple of years later, the second book about this 'bear of very little brain', *The House at Pooh Corner*, was published.

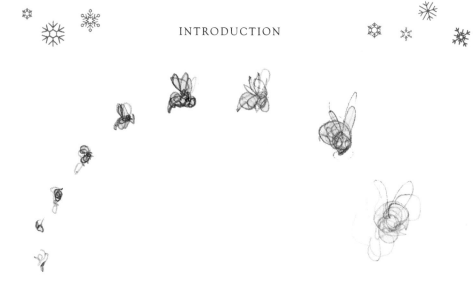

Inside this beautiful Winter Collection you will find two stories about Pooh from each book, as well as several carefully selected poems from A.A.Milne's two collections of verse, *When We Were Very Young,* and *Now We Are Six.* In addition you will find a very special Christmas illustration of Pooh and his friends that has never been published before.

All the pictures inside were drawn by E.H.Shepard and you can find out more about him, and A.A.Milne, at the back of the book.

Contents

"Do you think it's a
woosle?"

Pooh and Piglet
Go Hunting

The Piglet lived in a very grand house in the middle of a beech-tree, and the beech-tree was in the middle of the Forest, and the Piglet lived in the middle of the house. Next to his house was a piece of broken board which had: *'TRESPASSERS W'* on it. When Christopher Robin asked the Piglet what it meant, he said it was his grandfather's name, and had been in the family for a long time. Christopher Robin said you couldn't be called

Trespassers W, and Piglet said yes, you could, because his grandfather was, and it was short for Trespassers Will, which was short for Trespassers William. And his grandfather had had two names in case he lost one – Trespassers after an uncle, and William after Trespassers.

'I've got two names,' said Christopher Robin carelessly.

'Well, there you are, that proves it,' said Piglet.

One fine winter's day when Piglet was brushing away the snow in front of his house, he happened to look up, and there was Winnie-the-Pooh. Pooh was walking round and round in a circle, thinking of something else, and when Piglet called to him, he just went on walking.

'Hallo!' said Piglet, 'what are you doing?'

'Hunting,' said Pooh.

'Hunting what?'

'Tracking something,' said Winnie-the-Pooh very mysteriously.

'Tracking what?' said Piglet, coming closer.

'That's just what I ask myself. I ask myself, What?'

'What do you think you'll answer?'

'I shall have to wait until I catch up with it,' said Winnie-the-Pooh. 'Now, look there.' He pointed to the ground in front of him. 'What do you see there?'

'Tracks,' said Piglet. 'Paw-marks.' He gave a little squeak

*One fine winter's day when Piglet was brushing away
the snow in front of his house, he happened to look up,
and there was Winnie-the-Pooh.*

of excitement. 'Oh, Pooh! Do you think it's a – a – a Woozle?'

'It may be,' said Pooh. 'Sometimes it is, and sometimes it isn't. You never can tell with paw-marks.'

With these few words he went on tracking, and Piglet, after watching him for a minute or two, ran after him. Winnie-the-Pooh had come to a sudden stop, and was bending over the tracks in a puzzled sort of way.

'What's the matter?' asked Piglet.

'It's a very funny thing,' said Bear, 'but there seem to be two animals now. This – whatever-it-is – has been joined by another – whatever-it-is – and the two of them are now proceeding in company. Would you mind coming with me, Piglet, in case they turn out to be Hostile Animals?'

Piglet scratched his ear in a nice sort of way, and said that he had nothing to do until Friday, and would be delighted to come, in case it really was a Woozle.

*'Would you mind coming with me, Piglet, in case
they turn out to be Hostile Animals?'*

'You mean, in case it really is two Woozles,' said Winnie-the-Pooh, and Piglet said that anyhow he had nothing to do until Friday. So off they went together.

There was a small spinney of larch-trees just here, and it seemed as if the two Woozles, if that is what they were, had been going round this spinney; so round this spinney went Pooh and Piglet after them; Piglet passing the time by telling Pooh what his grandfather Trespassers W had done to Remove Stiffness after Tracking, and how his grandfather Trespassers W had suffered in his later years from Shortness of Breath, and other matters of interest, and Pooh wondering what a grandfather was like, and if perhaps this was Two Grandfathers they were after now, and, if so, whether he would be allowed to take one home and keep it, and what Christopher Robin would say. And still the tracks went on in front of them...

Suddenly Winnie-the-Pooh stopped, and pointed excitedly in front of him. 'Look!'

'What?' said Piglet, with a jump. And then, to show that he hadn't been frightened, he jumped up and down once or twice more in an exercising sort of way.

'The tracks!' said Pooh. 'A third animal has joined the other two!'

'Pooh!' cried Piglet. 'Do you think it is another Woozle?'

'No,' said Pooh, 'because it makes different marks. It is either Two Woozles and one, as it might be, Wizzle, or Two, as it might be, Wizzles and one, if so it is, Woozle. Let us continue to follow them.'

So they went on, feeling just a little anxious now, in case the three animals in front of them were of Hostile Intent. And Piglet wished very much that his grandfather

T. W. were there, instead of elsewhere, and Pooh thought how nice it would be if they met Christopher Robin suddenly but quite accidentally, and only because he liked Christopher Robin so much. And then, all of a sudden, Winnie-the-Pooh stopped again, and licked the tip of his nose in a cooling manner, for he was feeling more hot and anxious than ever in his life before. There were four animals in front of them!

'Do you see, Piglet? Look at their tracks! Three, as it were, Woozles, and one, as it was, Wizzle. Another Woozle has joined them!'

And so it seemed to be. There were the tracks; crossing over each other here, getting muddled up with each other there; but, quite plainly every now and then, the tracks of four sets of paws.

'I think,' said Piglet, when he had licked the tip of his nose too, and found that it brought very little comfort, 'I think that I have just remembered something. I have just remembered something that I forgot to do yesterday and shan't be able to do to-morrow. So I suppose I really ought to go back and do it now.'

'We'll do it this afternoon, and I'll come with you,' said Pooh.

'It isn't the sort of thing you can do in the afternoon,' said Piglet quickly. 'It's a very particular morning thing, that has to be done in the morning, and, if possible, between the hours of – What would you say the time was?'

'About twelve,' said Winnie-the-Pooh, looking at the sun.

'Between, as I was saying, the hours of twelve and twelve five. So, really, dear old Pooh, if you'll excuse me – What's that?'

Pooh looked up at the sky, and then, as he heard the whistle again, he looked up into the branches of a big oak-tree, and then he saw a friend of his.

'It's Christopher Robin,' he said.

'Ah, then you'll be all right,' said Piglet. 'You'll be quite safe with him. Good-bye,' and he trotted off home as quickly as he could, very glad to be Out of All Danger again. Christopher Robin came slowly down his tree.

'Silly old Bear,' he said, 'what were you doing? First you went round the spinney twice by yourself, and then Piglet ran after you and you went round again together, and then you were just going round a fourth time –'

'Wait a moment,' said Winnie-the-Pooh, holding up his paw.

He sat down and thought, in the most thoughtful way he could think. Then he fitted his paw into one of the Tracks ... and then he scratched his nose twice, and stood up.

'Yes,' said Winnie-the-Pooh.

'I see now,' said Winnie-the-Pooh.

'I have been Foolish and Deluded,' said he, 'and I am a Bear of No Brain at All.'

'You're the Best Bear in All the World,' said Christopher Robin soothingly.

'Am I?' said Pooh hopefully. And then he brightened up suddenly.

'Anyhow,' he said, 'it is nearly Luncheon Time.'

So he went home for it.

The End

Us Two

Wherever I am, there's always Pooh,
There's always Pooh and Me.
Whatever I do, he wants to do,
'Where are you going to-day?' says Pooh:
'Well, that's very odd 'cos I was too.
'Let's go together,' says Pooh, says he.
'Let's go together,' says Pooh.

'What's twice eleven?' I said to Pooh.
('Twice what?' said Pooh to Me.)
'I *think* it ought to be twenty-two.'
'Just what I think myself,' said Pooh.
'It wasn't an easy sum to do,
But that's what it is,' said Pooh, said he.
'That's what it is,' said Pooh.

'Let's look for dragons,' I said to Pooh.
'Yes, let's,' said Pooh to Me.
We crossed the river and found a few –
'Yes, those are dragons all right,' said Pooh.
'As soon as I saw their beaks I knew.
That's what they are,' said Pooh, said he.
'That's what they are,' said Pooh.
'Let's frighten the dragons,' I said to Pooh.
'That's right,' said Pooh to Me.

'*I'm* not afraid,' I said to Pooh,
And I held his paw and shouted 'Shoo!
Silly old dragons!' – and off they flew.
'I wasn't afraid,' said Pooh, said he,
'I'm *never* afraid with you.'

So wherever I am, there's always Pooh,
There's always Pooh and Me.
'What would I do?' I said to Pooh,
'If it wasn't for you,' and Pooh said: 'True,
It isn't much fun for One, but Two
Can stick together,' says Pooh, says he.
'That's how it is,' says Pooh.

"Help. its me"

EHShep

Piglet is Entirely Surrounded by Water

*I*t rained and it rained and it rained. Piglet told himself that never in all his life, and *he* was goodness knows *how* old – three, was it, or four? – never had he seen so much rain. Days and days and days.

'If only,' he thought, as he looked out of the window, 'I had been in Pooh's house, or Christopher Robin's house, or Rabbit's house when it began to rain, then I should have had Company all this time, instead of being here all alone, with nothing to do except wonder when it will stop.' And he imagined himself with Pooh, saying, 'Did you ever see such rain, Pooh?' and Pooh saying, 'Isn't it *awful*, Piglet?' and Piglet saying, 'I wonder how it is over Christopher Robin's way,' and Pooh saying, 'I should think poor old Rabbit is about flooded out by this time.' It would have been jolly to talk like this, and really, it wasn't much good having anything exciting like floods, if you couldn't share them with somebody.

For it was rather exciting. The little dry ditches in which Piglet had nosed about so often had become streams, the little streams across which he had splashed were rivers, and the river, between whose steep banks they had played so happily, had sprawled out of its own bed and was taking up so much room everywhere, that Piglet was beginning to wonder whether it would be coming into *his* bed soon.

'It's a little Anxious,' he said to himself, 'to be a Very Small Animal Entirely Surrounded by Water. Christopher Robin and Pooh could escape by Climbing Trees, and Kanga could escape by Jumping, and Rabbit could escape by Burrowing, and Owl could escape by Flying, and Eeyore could escape by – by Making a Loud Noise Until Rescued, and here am I, surrounded by water and I can't do *anything*.'

It went on raining, and every day the water got a little

'It's a little Anxious,' he said to himself, 'to be a Very Small
Animal Entirely Surrounded by Water.'

higher, until now it was nearly up to Piglet's window... and still he hadn't done anything.

'There's Pooh,' he thought to himself. 'Pooh hasn't much Brain, but he never comes to any harm. He does silly things and they turn out right. There's Owl. Owl hasn't exactly got Brain, but he Knows Things. He would know the Right Thing to Do when Surrounded by Water. There's Rabbit. He hasn't Learnt in Books, but he can always Think of a Clever Plan. There's Kanga. She isn't Clever, Kanga isn't, but she would be so anxious about Roo that she would do a Good Thing to Do without thinking about it. And then there's Eeyore. And Eeyore is so miserable anyhow that he wouldn't mind about this. But I wonder what Christopher Robin would do?'

Then suddenly he remembered a story which Christopher Robin had told him about a man on a desert island who had written something in a bottle and thrown it into the sea; and Piglet thought that if he wrote something in a bottle and threw it in the water, perhaps somebody would come and rescue *him!*

He left the window and began to search his house, all of it that wasn't under water, and at last he found a pencil and a small piece of dry paper, and a bottle with a cork to it. And he wrote on one side of the paper:

HELP!
PIGLIT (ME)

and on the other side:

IT'S ME PIGLIT, HELP HELP!

Then he put the paper in the bottle, and he corked the bottle up as tightly as he could, and he leant out of his window as far as he could lean without falling in, and he threw the bottle as far as he could throw – *splash!* – and in a little while it bobbed up again on the water; and he watched it floating slowly away in the distance, until his eyes ached with looking, and sometimes he thought it was the bottle, and sometimes he thought it was just a ripple on the water which he was following, and then suddenly he knew that he would never see it again and that he had done all that he could do to save himself.

'So now,' he thought, 'somebody else will have to do something, and I hope they will do it soon, because if they don't I shall have to swim, which I can't, so I hope they do it soon.' And then he gave a very long sigh and said, 'I wish Pooh were here. It's so much more friendly with two.'

When the rain began Pooh was asleep. It rained, and it rained, and it rained, and he slept and he slept and he slept. He had had a tiring day. You remember how he discovered the North Pole; well, he was so proud of this that he asked Christopher Robin if there were any other Poles such as a Bear of Little Brain might discover.

'There's a South Pole,' said Christopher Robin, 'and I expect there's an East Pole and a West Pole, though people don't like talking about them.'

Pooh was very excited when he heard this, and suggested that they should have an Expotition to discover the East Pole, but Christopher Robin had thought of something else to do with Kanga; so Pooh went out to discover the East Pole by himself. Whether he discovered it or not, I forget; but he was so tired when he got home that, in the very middle of his supper, after he had been eating for little

more than half-an-hour, he fell fast asleep in his chair, and slept and slept and slept.

Then suddenly he was dreaming. He was at the East Pole, and it was a very cold pole with the coldest sort of snow and ice all over it. He had found a beehive to sleep in, but there wasn't room for his legs, so he had left them outside. And Wild Woozles, such as inhabit the East Pole, came and nibbled all the fur off his legs to make Nests for their Young. And the more they nibbled, the colder his legs got, until suddenly he woke up with an *Ow!* – and there he was, sitting in his chair with his feet in the water, and water all round him!

He splashed to his door and looked out...

'This is Serious,' said Pooh. 'I must have an Escape.'

So he took his largest pot of honey and escaped with it to a broad branch of his tree, well above the water, and then he climbed down again and escaped with another pot ...and when the whole Escape was finished, there was Pooh sitting on his branch, dangling his legs, and there, beside him, were ten pots of honey...

Two days later, there was Pooh, sitting on his branch, dangling his legs, and there, beside him, were four pots of honey...

Three days later, there was Pooh, sitting on his branch, dangling his legs, and there beside him, was one pot of honey.

Four days later, there was Pooh...

And it was on the morning of the fourth day that Piglet's bottle came floating past him, and with one loud cry of 'Honey!' Pooh plunged into the water, seized the bottle, and struggled back to his tree again.

'Bother!' said Pooh, as he opened it. 'All that wet for nothing. What's that bit of paper doing?'

He took it out and looked at it.

'It's a Missage,' he said to himself, 'that's what it is. And that letter is a 'P', and so is that, and so is that, and 'P' means 'Pooh', so it's a very important Missage to me, and I can't read it. I must find Christopher Robin or Owl or Piglet, one of those Clever Readers who can read things, and they will tell me what this missage means. Only I can't swim. Bother!'

Then he had an idea, and I think that for a Bear of Very Little Brain, it was a good idea. He said to himself:

'If a bottle can float, then a jar can float, and if a jar floats, I can sit on the top of it, if it's a very big jar.'

So he took his biggest jar, and corked it up.

'All boats have to have a name,' he said, 'so I shall call mine *The Floating Bear*.' And with these words he dropped his boat into the water and jumped in after it.

For a little while Pooh and *The Floating Bear* were uncertain as to which of them was meant to be on the top,

but after trying one or two different positions,

they settled down with *The Floating Bear* underneath and Pooh triumphantly astride it, paddling vigorously with his feet.

Christopher Robin lived at the very top of the Forest. It rained, and it rained, and it rained, but the water couldn't come up to *his* house. It was rather jolly to look down into the valleys and see the water all round him, but it rained so hard that he stayed indoors most of the time, and thought about things. Every morning he went out with his umbrella and put a stick in the place where the water came up to, and every next morning he went out and couldn't see his stick any more, so he put another stick in the place where the water came up to, and then he walked home again, and each morning he had a shorter way to walk than he had had the morning before. On the morning of the fifth day he saw the water all round him, and knew that for the first time in his life he was on a real island. Which was very exciting.

It was on this morning that Owl came flying over the water to say 'How do you do?' to his friend Christopher Robin.

'I say, Owl,' said Christopher Robin, 'isn't this fun? I'm on an island!'

'The atmospheric conditions have been very unfavourable lately,' said Owl.

'The what?'

'It has been raining,' explained Owl.

*Every morning he went out with his umbrella and put a
stick in the place where the water came up to.*

'Yes,' said Christopher Robin. 'It has.'

'The flood-level has reached an unprecedented height.'

'The who?'

'There's a lot of water about,' explained Owl.

'Yes,' said Christopher Robin, 'there is.'

'However, the prospects are rapidly becoming more favourable. At any moment –'

'Have you seen Pooh?'

'No. At any moment –'

'I hope he's all right,' said Christopher Robin. 'I've been wondering about him. I expect Piglet's with him. Do you think they're all right, Owl?'

'I expect so. You see, at any moment –'

'Do go and see, Owl. Because Pooh hasn't got very much brain, and he might do something silly, and I do love him so, Owl. Do you see, Owl?'

'That's all right,' said Owl. 'I'll go. Back directly.' And he flew off.

In a little while he was back again.

'Pooh isn't there,' he said.

'Not there?'

'He's *been* there. He's been sitting on a branch of his tree outside his house with nine pots of honey. But he isn't

there now.'

'Oh, Pooh!' cried Christopher Robin. 'Where *are* you?'

'Here I am,' said a growly voice behind him.

'Pooh!'

They rushed into each other's arms.

'How did you get here, Pooh?' asked Christopher Robin, when he was ready to talk again.

'On my boat,' said Pooh proudly. 'I had a Very Important Missage sent me in a bottle, and owing to having got some water in my eyes, I couldn't read it, so I brought it to you. On my boat.'

With these proud words he gave Christopher Robin the missage.

'But it's from Piglet!' cried Christopher Robin when he had read it.

'Isn't there anything about Pooh in it?' asked Bear, looking over his shoulder.

Christopher Robin read the message aloud.

'Oh, are those "P's" piglets? I thought they were pooh's.'

'We must rescue him at once! I thought he was with you, Pooh. Owl, could you rescue him on your back?'

'I don't think so,' said Owl, after grave thought. 'It is doubtful if the necessary dorsal muscles –'

'Then would you fly to him at *once* and say that Rescue

is Coming? And Pooh and I will think of a Rescue and come as quick as ever we can. Oh, don't *talk*, Owl, go on quick!' And, still thinking of something to say, Owl flew off.

'Now then, Pooh,' said Christopher Robin, 'where's your boat?'

'I ought to say,' explained Pooh as they walked down to

the shore of the island, 'that it isn't just an ordinary sort of boat. Sometimes it's a Boat, and sometimes it's more of an Accident. It all depends.'

'Depends on what?'

'On whether I'm on the top of it or underneath it.'

'Oh! Well, where is it?'

'There!' said Pooh, pointing proudly to *The Floating Bear*.

It wasn't what Christopher Robin expected, and the

more he looked at it, the more he thought what a Brave and Clever Bear Pooh was, and the more Christopher Robin thought this, the more Pooh looked modestly down his nose and tried to pretend he wasn't.

'But it's too small for two of us,' said Christopher Robin sadly.

'Three of us with Piglet.'

'That makes it smaller still. Oh, Pooh Bear, what shall we do?'

And then this Bear, Pooh Bear, Winnie-the-Pooh, F. O. P. (Friend of Piglet's), R. C. (Rabbit's Companion), P. D. (Pole Discoverer), E. C. and T. F. (Eeyore's Comforter and Tail-finder) – in fact, Pooh himself – said something so clever that Christopher Robin could only look at him with mouth open and eyes staring, wondering if this was really the Bear of Very Little Brain whom he had known and loved so long.

'We might go in your umbrella,' said Pooh.

'?'

'We might go in your umbrella,' said Pooh.

'? ?'

'We might go in your umbrella,' said Pooh.

'! ! ! ! ! !'

For suddenly Christopher Robin saw that they might.

'We might go in your umbrella,' said Pooh.

He opened his umbrella and put it point downwards in the water. It floated but wobbled. Pooh got in.

He was just beginning to say that it was all right now, when he found that it wasn't, so after a short drink, which he didn't really want, he waded back to Christopher Robin. Then they both got in together, and it wobbled no longer.

'I shall call this boat *The Brain of Pooh*,' said Christopher Robin, and *The Brain of Pooh* set sail forthwith in a south-westerly direction, revolving gracefully.

You can imagine Piglet's joy when at last the ship came in sight of him. In after-years he liked to think that he had been in Very Great Danger during the Terrible Flood, but the only danger he had really been in was the last half-hour of his imprisonment, when Owl, who had just flown up, sat on a branch of his tree to comfort him, and told him a very long story about an aunt who had once laid a seagull's egg by mistake, and the story went on and on, rather like this sentence, until Piglet who was listening out of his window without much hope, went to sleep quietly and naturally, slipping slowly out of the window towards the water until he was only hanging on by his toes, at which moment, luckily, a sudden loud squawk from Owl, which was really part of the story, being what his aunt said, woke the Piglet up and just gave him time to jerk himself back

into safety and say, 'How interesting, and did she?' when – well, you can imagine his joy when at last he saw the good ship, *Brain of Pooh* (*Captain*, C. Robin; *1st Mate*, P. Bear) coming over the sea to rescue him…

And as that is really the end of the story, and I am very tired after that last sentence, I think I shall stop there.

The End

Brain of Pooh (Captain, C. Robin; 1st Mate, P. Bear)

Waiting at the Window

These are my two drops of rain
Waiting on the window-pane.

I am waiting here to see
Which the winning one will be.
Both of them have different names.
One is John and one is James.

All the best and all the worst
Comes from which of them is first.

James has just begun to ooze.
He's the one I want to lose.

John is waiting to begin.
He's the one I want to win.

James is going slowly on.
Something sort of sticks to John.

John is moving off at last.
James is going pretty fast.

John is rushing down the pane.
James is going slow again.

James has met a sort of smear.
John is getting very near.
Is he going fast enough?
(James has found a piece of fluff.)

John has hurried quickly by.
(James was talking to a fly.)

John is there, and John has won!
Look! I told you! Here's the sun!

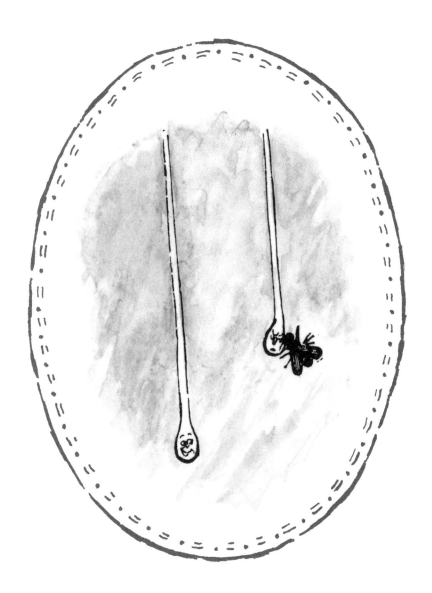

The Friend

There are lots and lots of people who are always asking things,
Like Dates and Pounds-and-ounces and the names of funny Kings,
And the answer's either Sixpence or A Hundred Inches Long,
And I know they'll think me silly if I get the answer wrong.

So Pooh and I go whispering, and Pooh looks very bright,
And says, 'Well, I say sixpence, but I don't suppose I'm right.'
And then it doesn't matter what the answer ought to be,
'Cos if he's right, I'm Right, and if he's wrong, it isn't Me.

The Engineer

Let it rain!
Who cares?
I've a train
Upstairs,
With a brake
Which I make
From a string
Sort of thing,
Which works
In jerks,
'Cos it drops
In the spring,
Which stops
With the string,

And the wheels
All stick
So quick
That it feels
Like a thing
That you make
With a brake,
Not string...

So that's what I make,
When the day's all wet.
It's a good sort of brake
But it hasn't worked yet.

A House is Built at Pooh Corner for Eeyore

One day when Pooh Bear had nothing else to do, he thought he would do something, so he went round to Piglet's house to see what Piglet was doing. It was still snowing as he stumped over the white forest track, and he expected to find Piglet warming his toes in front of his fire, but to his surprise he saw that the door was open, and the more he looked inside the more Piglet wasn't there.

'He's out,' said Pooh sadly. 'That's what it is. He's not in. I shall have to go a fast Thinking Walk by myself. Bother!'

But first he thought that he would knock very loudly just to make quite sure ... and while he waited for Piglet not to answer, he jumped up and down to keep warm, and a hum came suddenly into his head, which seemed to him a Good Hum, such as is Hummed Hopefully to Others.

> The more it snows
>   (Tiddely pom),
> The more it goes
>   (Tiddely pom),
> The more it goes
>   (Tiddely pom),
> On snowing.
> And nobody knows
>   (Tiddely pom),
> How cold my toes
>   (Tiddely pom),
> How cold my toes
>   (Tiddely pom),
> Are growing.

'So what I'll do,' said Pooh, 'is I'll do this. I'll just go home first and see what the time is, and perhaps I'll put a muffler round my neck, and then I'll go and see Eeyore and sing it to him.'

He hurried back to his own house; and his mind was so busy on the way with the hum that he was getting ready for Eeyore that, when he suddenly saw Piglet

sitting in his best arm-chair, he could only stand there rubbing his head and wondering whose house he was in.

'Hallo, Piglet,' he said. 'I thought you were out.'

'No,' said Piglet, 'it's you who were out, Pooh.'

'So it was,' said Pooh. 'I knew one of us was.'

He looked up at his clock, which had stopped at five minutes to eleven some weeks ago.

'Nearly eleven o'clock,' said Pooh happily. 'You're just in time for a little smackerel of something,' and he put his head into the cupboard. 'And then we'll go out, Piglet, and sing my song to Eeyore.'

'Which song, Pooh?'

'The one we're going to sing to Eeyore,' explained Pooh.

The clock was still saying five minutes to eleven when Pooh and Piglet set out on their way half an hour later. The wind had dropped, and the snow, tired of rushing round in circles trying to catch itself up, now fluttered gently down until it found a place on which to rest, and sometimes the place was Pooh's nose and sometimes it wasn't, and in a little while Piglet was wearing a white muffler round his neck and feeling more snowy behind the ears than he had ever felt before.

'Pooh,' he said at last, and a little timidly, because he didn't want Pooh to think he was Giving In, 'I was

just wondering. How would it be if we went home now and practised your song, and then sang it to Eeyore tomorrow – or – or the next day, when we happen to see him?'

'That's a very good idea, Piglet,' said Pooh. 'We'll practise it now as we go along. But it's no good going home to practise it, because it's a special Outdoor Song which Has To Be Sung In The Snow.'

'Are you sure?' asked Piglet anxiously.

'Well, you'll see, Piglet, when you listen. Because this is how it begins. The more it snows, tiddely pom –'

'Tiddely what?' said Piglet.

'Pom,' said Pooh. 'I put that in to make it more hummy. The more it goes, tiddely pom, the more –

'Didn't you say snows?'

'Yes, but that was before.'

'Before the tiddely pom?'

'It was a different tiddely pom,' said Pooh, feeling rather muddled now. 'I'll sing it to you properly and then you'll see.'

So he sang it again.

The more it
SNOWS~tiddely~pom
The more it
GOES~tiddely~pom
The more it
GOES~tiddely~pom

On
Snowing.
And nobody
KNOWS-tiddely-pom,
How cold my
TOES-tiddely-pom
How cold my
TOESS-tiddely-pom
Are
Growing.

He sang it like that, which is much the best way of singing it, and when he had finished, he waited for Piglet to say that, of all the Outdoor Hums for Snowy Weather he had ever heard, this was the best. And, after thinking the matter out carefully, Piglet said:

'Pooh,' he said solemnly, 'it isn't the toes so much as the ears.'

By this time they were getting near Eeyore's Gloomy Place, which was where he lived, and as it was still very snowy behind Piglet's ears, and he was getting tired of it, they turned into a little pine-wood, and sat down on the gate which led into it. They were out of the snow now, but it was very cold, and to keep themselves warm

they sang Pooh's song right through six times, Piglet doing the tiddely-poms and Pooh doing the rest of it, and both of them thumping on the top of the gate with pieces of stick at the proper places. And in a little while they felt much warmer, and were able to talk again.

'I've been thinking,' said Pooh, 'and what I've been

thinking about is this. I've been thinking about Eeyore.'

'What about Eeyore?'

'Well, poor Eeyore has nowhere to live.'

'Nor he has,' said Piglet.

'You have a house, Piglet, and I have a house, and they are very good houses. And Christopher Robin has a house, and Owl and Kanga and Rabbit have houses, and even Rabbit's friends and relations have houses or somethings, but poor Eeyore has nothing. So what I've been thinking is: Let's build him a house.'

'That,' said Piglet, 'is a Grand Idea. Where shall we build it?'

'We will build it here,' said Pooh, 'just by this wood, out of the wind, because this is where I thought of it. And we will call this Pooh Corner. And we will build an Eeyore House with sticks at Pooh Corner for Eeyore.'

'There was a heap of sticks on the other side of the wood,' said Piglet. 'I saw them. Lots and lots. All piled up.'

'Thank you, Piglet,' said Pooh. 'What you have just said will be a Great Help to us, and because of it I could call this place Poohanpiglet Corner if Pooh Corner didn't sound better, which it does, being smaller and more like a corner. Come along.'

So they got down off the gate and went round to the other side of the wood to fetch the sticks.

Christopher Robin had spent the morning indoors going to Africa and back, and he had just got off the boat and was wondering what it was like outside, when who should come knocking at the door but Eeyore.

'Hallo, Eeyore,' said Christopher Robin, as he opened the door and came out. 'How are you?'

'It's snowing still,' said Eeyore gloomily.

'So it is.'

'And freezing.'

'Is it?'

'Yes,' said Eeyore. 'However,' he said, brightening up a little, 'we haven't had an earthquake lately.'

'What's the matter, Eeyore?'

'Nothing, Christopher Robin. Nothing important. I suppose you haven't seen a house or what-not anywhere about?'

'What sort of a house?'

'Just a house.'

'Who lives there?'

'I do. At least I thought I did. But I suppose I don't. After all, we can't all have houses.'

'But, Eeyore, I didn't know – I always thought –'

'I don't know how it is, Christopher Robin, but what with all this snow and one thing and another, not to mention icicles and such-ike, it isn't so Hot in my field about three o'clock in the morning as some people think it is. It isn't Close, if you know what I mean – not so as to be uncomfortable. It isn't Stuffy. In fact, Christopher Robin,' he went on in a loud whisper, 'quite-be-tween-our-selves-and-don't-tell-anybody, it's Cold.'

'Oh, Eeyore!'

'And I said to myself: The others will be sorry if I'm getting myself all cold. They haven't got Brains, any of them, only grey fluff that's blown into their heads by mistake, and they don't Think, but if it goes on snowing for another six weeks or so, one of them will begin to say to himself: "Eeyore can't be so very much too Hot about three o'clock in the morning." And then it will Get About. And they'll be Sorry.'

'Oh, Eeyore!' said Christopher Robin, feeling very sorry already.

'I don't mean you, Christopher Robin. You're different. So what it all comes to is that I built myself a house down by my little wood.'

'Did you really? How exciting!'

'The really exciting part,' said Eeyore in his most melancholy voice, 'is that when I left it this morning it was there, and when I came back it wasn't. Not at all, very natural, and it was only Eeyore's house. But still I just wondered.'

Christopher Robin didn't stop to wonder. He was already back in his house, putting on his waterproof hat, his waterproof boots, and his waterproof macintosh as fast as he could.

'We'll go and look for it at once,' he called out to Eeyore.

'Sometimes,' said Eeyore, 'when people have quite finished taking a person's house, there are one or two bits which they don't want and are rather glad for the person to take back, if you know what I mean. So I thought if we just went –'

'Come on,' said Christopher Robin, and off they hurried, and in a very little time they got to the corner of the field by the side of the pine-wood, where Eeyore's house wasn't any longer.

'There!' said Eeyore. 'Not a stick of it left! Of course, I've still got all this snow to do what I like with. One mustn't complain.'

But Christopher Robin wasn't listening to Eeyore, he was listening to something else.

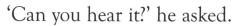
'Can you hear it?' he asked.

'What is it? Somebody laughing?'

'Listen.'

They both listened ... and they heard a deep gruff voice saying in a singing voice that the more it snowed the more it went on snowing, and a small high voice tiddely-pomming in between.

'It's Pooh,' said Christopher Robin excitedly...

'Possibly,' said Eeyore.

'And Piglet!' said Christopher Robin excitedly.

'Probably,' said Eeyore. 'What we want is a Trained Bloodhound.'

The words of the song changed suddenly.

'We've finished our HOUSE!' sang the gruff voice.

'Tiddely pom!' sang the squeaky one.

'It's a beautiful HOUSE…'

'Tiddely pom…'

'I wish it were MINE…'

'Tiddely pom…'

'Pooh!' shouted Christopher Robin…

The singers on the gate stopped suddenly.

'It's Christopher Robin!' said Pooh eagerly.

'He's round by the place where we got all those sticks from,' said Piglet.

'Come on,' said Pooh.

They climbed down their gate and hurried round the corner of the wood, Pooh making welcoming noises all the way.

'Why, here is Eeyore,' said Pooh, when he had finished hugging Christopher Robin, and he nudged Piglet, and Piglet nudged him, and they thought to themselves what a lovely surprise they had got ready. 'Hallo, Eeyore.'

'Same to you, Pooh Bear, and twice on Thursdays,' said Eeyore gloomily.

Before Pooh could say: 'Why Thursdays?' Christopher Robin began to explain the sad story of Eeyore's Lost

House. And Pooh and Piglet listened, and their eyes seemed to get bigger and bigger.

'Where did you say it was?' asked Pooh.

'Just here,' said Eeyore.

'Made of sticks?'

'Yes.'

'Oh!' said Piglet.

'What?' said Eeyore.

'I just said "Oh!"' said Piglet nervously. And so as to seem quite at ease he hummed tiddely-pom once or twice in a what-shall-we-do-now kind of way.

'You're sure it was a house?' said Pooh. 'I mean, you're sure the house was just here?'

'Of course I am,' said Eeyore. And he murmured to himself, 'No brain at all, some of them.'

'Why, what's the matter, Pooh?' asked Christopher Robin.

'Well,' said Pooh... 'The fact is,' said Pooh...

'Well, the fact is,' said Pooh... 'You see,' said Pooh...

'It's like this,' said Pooh, and something seemed to tell him that he wasn't explaining very well, and he nudged Piglet again.

'It's like this,' said Piglet quickly... 'Only warmer,' he added after deep thought.

'What's warmer?'

'The other side of the wood, where Eeyore's house is.'

'My house?' said Eeyore. 'My house was here.'

'No,' said Piglet firmly. 'The other side of the wood.'

'Because of being warmer,' said Pooh.

'But I ought to know –'

'Come and look,' said Piglet simply, and he led the way.

'There wouldn't be two houses,' said Pooh. 'Not so close together.'

They came round the corner, and there was Eeyore's house, looking as comfy as anything.

'There you are,' said Piglet.

'Inside as well as outside,' said Pooh proudly.

Eeyore went inside…and came out again.

'It's a remarkable thing,' he said. 'It is my house, and I built it where I said I did, so the wind must have blown it here. And the wind blew it right over the wood, and blew it down here, and here it is as good as ever. In fact, better in places.'

'Much better,' said Pooh and Piglet together.

'It just shows what can be done by taking a little trouble,' said Eeyore. 'Do you see, Pooh? Do you see, Piglet? Brains first and then Hard Work. Look at it! That's the way to build a house,' said Eeyore proudly.

So they left him in it; and Christopher Robin went back to lunch with his friends Pooh and Piglet, and on the way they told him of the Awful Mistake they had made. And when he had finished laughing, they all sang the Outdoor Song for Snowy Weather the rest of the way home, Piglet, who was still not quite sure of his voice, putting in the tiddely-poms again.

'And I know it seems easy,' said Piglet to himself, 'but it isn't every one who could do it.'

The End

Sneezles

Christopher Robin
Had wheezles
And sneezles,
They bundled him
Into
His bed.
They gave him what goes
With a cold in the nose,
And some more for a cold
In the head.
They wondered
If wheezles
Could turn
Into measles,
If sneezles
Would turn
Into mumps;

They examined his chest
For a rash,
And the rest
Of his body for swellings and lumps.
They sent for some doctors
In sneezles
And wheezles
To tell them what ought
To be done.

All sorts and conditions
Of famous physicians
Came hurrying round
At a run.
They all made a note
Of the state of his throat,

They asked if he suffered from thirst;
They asked if the sneezles
Came *after* the wheezles,
Or if the first sneezle
Came first.
They said, 'If you teazle
A sneezle
Or wheezle,
A measle
May easily grow.
But humour or pleazle
The wheezle
Or sneezle,
The measle
Will certainly go.'
They expounded the reazles
For sneezles
And wheezles,
The manner of measles
When new.
They said 'If he freezles
In draughts and in breezles,
Then PHTHEEZLES
May even ensue.'

Christopher Robin
Got up in the morning,
The sneezles had vanished away.
And the look in his eye
Seemed to say to the sky,
'Now, how to amuse them to-day?'

"Holding on to Each other".

(A very Grand time,)

Piglet Does a Very Grand Thing

Half-way between Pooh's house and Piglet's house was a Thoughtful Spot where they met sometimes when they had decided to go and see each other, and as it was warm and out of the wind they would sit down there for a little and wonder what they would do now that they had seen each other. One day when they had decided not to do anything, Pooh made up a verse about it, so that everybody should know what the place was for.

This warm and sunny Spot
Belongs to Pooh.
And here he wonders what
He's going to do.
Oh, bother, I forgot –
It's Piglet's too.

Now one autumn morning when the wind had blown all the leaves off the trees in the night, and was trying to blow the branches off, Pooh and Piglet were sitting in the Thoughtful Spot and wondering.

'What I think,' said Pooh, 'is I think we'll go to Pooh Corner and see Eeyore, because perhaps his house has been blown down, and perhaps he'd like us to build it again.'

'What I think,' said Piglet, 'is I think we'll go and see Christopher Robin, only he won't be there, so we can't.'

'Let's go and see everybody,' said Pooh. 'Because when you've been walking in the wind for miles, and you suddenly go into somebody's house, and he says, "Hallo, Pooh, you're just in time for a little smackerel of something," and you are, then it's what I call a Friendly Day.'

Piglet thought that they ought to have a Reason for going to see everybody, like Looking for Small or Organizing an Expotition, if Pooh could think of something.

Pooh could.

'We'll go because it's Thursday,' he said, 'and we'll go to wish everybody a Very Happy Thursday. Come on, Piglet.'

They got up; and when Piglet had sat down again, because he didn't know the wind was so strong, and had been helped up by Pooh, they started off. They went to

Pooh's house first, and luckily Pooh was at home just as they got there, so he asked them in, and they had some, and then they went on to Kanga's house, holding on to each other, and shouting, 'Isn't it?' and 'What?' and 'I can't hear.' By the time they got to Kanga's house they were so buffeted that they stayed to lunch. Just at first it seemed rather cold outside afterwards, so they pushed on to Rabbit's as quickly as they could.

'We've come to wish you a Very Happy Thursday,' said Pooh, when he had gone in and out once or twice just to make sure that he could get out again.

'Why, what's going to happen on Thursday?' asked Rabbit, and when Pooh had explained, and Rabbit, whose life was made up of Important Things, said, 'Oh, I thought you'd really come about something,' they sat down for a little... and by-and-by Pooh and Piglet went on again. The wind was behind them now, so they didn't have to shout.

'Rabbit's clever,' said Pooh thoughtfully.

'Yes,' said Piglet, 'Rabbit's clever.'

'And he has Brain.'

'Yes,' said Piglet, 'Rabbit has Brain.'

There was a long silence.

'I suppose,' said Pooh, 'that that's why he never understands anything.'

Christopher Robin was at home by this time, because it was the afternoon, and he was so glad to see them that they stayed there until very nearly tea-time, and then they had a Very Nearly tea, which is one you forget about afterwards, and hurried on to Pooh Corner, so as to see Eeyore before it was too late to have a Proper Tea with Owl.

'Hallo, Eeyore,' they called out cheerfully.

'Ah!' said Eeyore. 'Lost your way?'

'We just came to see you,' said Piglet. 'And to see how your house was. Look, Pooh, it's still standing!'

'I know,' said Eeyore. 'Very odd. Somebody ought to have come down and pushed it over.'

'We wondered whether the wind would blow it down,' said Pooh.

'Ah, that's why nobody's bothered, I suppose. I thought perhaps they'd forgotten.'

'Well, we're very glad to see you, Eeyore, and now we're going on to see Owl.'

'That's right. You'll like Owl. He flew past a day or two ago and noticed me. He didn't actually say anything, mind you, but he knew it was me. Very friendly of him, I thought. Encouraging.'

Pooh and Piglet shuffled about a little and said, 'Well, good-bye, Eeyore,' as lingeringly as they could, but they had a long way to go, and wanted to be getting on.

'Good-bye,' said Eeyore. 'Mind you don't get blown away, little Piglet. You'd be missed. People would say, "Where's little Piglet been blown to?" – really wanting to know. Well, good-bye. And thank you for happening to pass me.'

'Good-bye,' said Pooh and Piglet for the last time, and they pushed on to Owl's house.

The wind was against them now, and Piglet's ears

streamed behind him

like banners

as he fought his way along,

and it seemed hours before he got them into the shelter of the Hundred Acre Wood and they stood up straight again, to listen, a little nervously, to the roaring of the gale among the tree-tops.

'Supposing a tree fell down, Pooh, when we were underneath it?'

'Supposing it didn't,' said Pooh after careful thought.

Piglet was comforted by this, and in a little while they were knocking and ringing very cheerfully at Owl's door.

'Hallo, Owl,' said Pooh. 'I hope we're not too late for – I mean, how are you, Owl? Piglet and I just came to see how you were because it's Thursday.'

'Sit down, Pooh, sit down, Piglet,' said Owl kindly. 'Make yourselves comfortable.'

They thanked him, and made themselves as comfortable as they could.

'Because, you see, Owl,' said Pooh, 'we've been hurrying, so as to be in time for – so as to see you before we went away again.'

Owl nodded solemnly.

'Correct me if I am wrong,' he said, 'but am I right in supposing that it is a very Blusterous day outside?'

'Very,' said Piglet, who was quietly thawing his ears, and wishing that he was safely back in his own house.

... in a little while they were knocking and ringing very cheerfully at Owl's door.

'I thought so,' said Owl. 'It was on just such a blusterous day as this that my Uncle Robert, a portrait of whom you see upon the wall on your right, Piglet, while returning in the late forenoon from a – What's that?'

There was a loud cracking noise.

'Look out!' cried Pooh. 'Mind the clock! Out of the way, Piglet! Piglet, I'm falling on you!'

'Help!' cried Piglet.

Pooh's side of the room was slowly tilting upwards and his chair began sliding down on Piglet's. The clock slithered gently along the mantelpiece, collecting vases on the way, until they all crashed together on to what had once

been the floor, but was now trying to see what it looked like as a wall. Uncle Robert, who was going to be the new hearthrug, and was bringing the rest of his wall with him as carpet, met Piglet's chair just as Piglet was expecting to leave it, and for a little while it became very difficult to remember which was really the north. Then there was another loud crack...Owl's room collected itself feverishly ...and there was silence.

In a corner of the room, the table~cloth began to wriggle.

Then it wrapped itself into a ball and rolled

across the room.

Then it jumped up and down

once or twice, and put out
two ears.

It rolled across the room
again, and unwound itself.

'Pooh,' said Piglet nervously.

'Yes,' said one of the chairs.

'Where are we?'

'I'm not quite sure,' said the chair.

'Are we – are we in Owl's House?'

'I think so, because we were just going to have tea, and
we hadn't had it.'

'Oh!' said Piglet. 'Well, did Owl always have a letter-box
in his ceiling?'

'Has he?'

'Yes, look.'

'I can't,' said Pooh. 'I'm face downwards under
something, and that, Piglet, is a very bad position for
looking at ceilings.'

'Well, he has, Pooh.'

'Perhaps he's changed it,' said Pooh. 'Just for a change.'

There was a disturbance behind the table in the other corner of the room, and Owl was with them again.

'Ah, Piglet,' said Owl, looking very much annoyed; 'where's Pooh?'

'I'm not quite sure,' said Pooh.

Owl turned at his voice, and frowned at as much of Pooh as he could see.

'Pooh,' said Owl severely, 'did you do that?'

'No,' said Pooh humbly. 'I don't think so.'

'Then who did?'

'I think it was the wind,' said Piglet. 'I think your house has blown down.'

'Oh, is that it? I thought it was Pooh.'

'No,' said Pooh.

'If it was the wind,' said Owl, considering the matter, 'then it wasn't Pooh's fault. No blame can be attached to him.' With these kind words he flew up to look at his new ceiling.

'Piglet!' called Pooh in a loud whisper.

Piglet leant down to him.

'Yes, Pooh?'

'What did he say was attached to me?'

'He said he didn't blame you.'

'Oh! I thought he meant – Oh, I see.'

'Owl,' said Piglet, 'come down and help Pooh.'

Owl, who was admiring his letter-box, flew down again. Together they pushed and pulled at the armchair, and in a little while Pooh came out from underneath, and was able to look round him again.

'Well!' said Owl. 'This is a nice state of things!'

'What are we going to do, Pooh? Can you think of anything?' asked Piglet.

'Well, I had just thought of something,' said Pooh. 'It was just a little thing I thought of.' And he began to sing:

> I lay on my chest
> And I thought it best
> To pretend I was having an evening rest;
> I lay on my tum
> And I tried to hum
> But nothing particular seemed to come.
> My face was flat
> On the floor, and that
> Is all very well for an acrobat;
> But it doesn't seem fair
> To a Friendly Bear
> To stiffen him out with a basket~chair.
> And a sort of sqoze
> Which grows and grows
> Is not too nice for his poor old nose,
> And a sort of squch
> Is much too much
> For his neck and his mouth and his ears and such.

'That was all,' said Pooh.

Owl coughed in an unadmiring sort of way, and said

that, if Pooh was sure that was all, they could now give their minds to the Problem of Escape.

'Because,' said Owl, 'we can't go out by what used to be the front door. Something's fallen on it.'

'But how else can you go out?' asked Piglet anxiously.

'That is the Problem, Piglet, to which I am asking Pooh to give his mind.'

Pooh sat on the floor which had once been a wall, and gazed up at the ceiling which had once been another wall, with a front door in it which had once been a front door, and tried to give his mind to it.

'Could you fly up to the letter-box with Piglet on your back?' he asked.

'No,' said Piglet quickly. 'He couldn't.'

Owl explained about the Necessary Dorsal Muscles. He had explained this to Pooh and Christopher Robin once before, and had been waiting ever since for a chance to do it again, because it is a thing which you can easily explain twice before anybody knows what you are talking about.

'Because you see, Owl, if we could get Piglet into the letter-box, he might squeeze through the place where the letters come, and climb down the tree and run for help.'

Piglet said hurriedly that he had been getting bigger lately, and couldn't possibly, much as he would like to, and Owl said that he had had his letter-box made bigger lately in case he got bigger letters, so perhaps Piglet might, and Piglet said, 'But you said the necessary you-know-whats wouldn't,' and Owl said, 'No, they won't, so it's no good thinking about it,' and Piglet said, 'Then we'd better think of something else,' and began to at once.

But Pooh's mind had gone back to the day when he had saved Piglet from the flood, and everybody had admired him so much; and as that didn't often happen, he thought he would like it to happen again. And suddenly, just as it had come before, an idea came to him.

'Owl,' said Pooh, 'I have thought of something.'

'Astute and Helpful Bear,' said Owl.

Pooh looked proud at being called a stout and helpful bear, and said modestly that he just happened to think of it. You tied a piece of string to Piglet, and you flew up to the letter-box, with the other end in your beak, and you pushed it through the wire and brought it down to the floor, and you and Pooh pulled hard at this end, and Piglet went slowly up at the other end. And there you were.

'And there Piglet is,' said Owl. 'If the string doesn't break.'

'Supposing it does?' asked Piglet, really wanting to know.

'Then we try another piece of string.'

This was not very comforting to Piglet, because however many pieces of string they tried pulling up with, it would always be the same him coming down; but still, it did seem the only thing to do. So with one last look back in his mind at all the happy hours he had spent in the Forest not being pulled up to the ceiling by a piece of string, Piglet nodded bravely at Pooh and said that it was a Very Clever pup-pup-pup Clever pup-pup Plan.

'It won't break,' whispered Pooh comfortingly, 'because you're a Small Animal, and I'll stand underneath, and if you save us all, it will be a Very Grand Thing to talk about

afterwards, and perhaps I'll make up a Song, and people will say, "It was so grand what Piglet did that a Respectful Pooh Song was made about it!"'

Piglet felt much better after this, and when everything was ready, and he found himself slowly going up to the ceiling, he was so proud that he would have called out 'Look at me!'

if he hadn't been afraid that Pooh and Owl would let go of their end of the string and look at him.

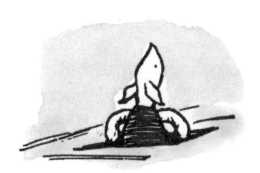

'Up we go!' said Pooh cheerfully.

'The ascent is proceeding as expected,' said Owl helpfully. Soon it was over. Piglet opened the letter-box and climbed in. Then, having untied himself, he began to squeeze into the slit, through which in the old days when front doors were front doors, many an unexpected letter that WOL had written to himself, had come slipping.

He squeezed and he sqoze, and then with one last squze he was out. Happy and excited he turned round to squeak a last message to the prisoners.

'It's all right,' he called through the letter-box. 'Your tree is blown right over, Owl, and there's a branch across the door, but Christopher Robin and I can move it, and we'll bring a rope for Pooh, and I'll go and tell him now, and I can climb down quite easily, I mean it's dangerous but I can do it all right, and Christopher Robin and I will be back in about half an hour. Good-bye, Pooh!' And without waiting to hear Pooh's answering 'Good-bye, and thank you, Piglet,' he was off.

'Half an hour,' said Owl, settling himself comfortably. 'That will just give me time to finish that story I was telling you about my Uncle Robert – a portrait of whom you see underneath you. Now let me see, where was I? Oh, yes. It was on just such a blusterous day as this that my Uncle Robert –'

Pooh closed his eyes.

The End

Wind on the Hill

No one can tell me,
  Nobody knows,
Where the wind comes from,
  Where the wind goes.

It's flying from somewhere
    As fast as it can,
I couldn't keep up with it,
    Not if I ran.

But if I stopped holding
    The string of my kite,
It would blow with the wind
    For a day and a night.

And then when I found it,
    Wherever it blew,
I should know that the wind
    Had been going there too.

So then I could tell them
    Where the wind goes...
But where the wind comes from
    Nobody knows.

Happiness

John had
Great Big
Waterproof
Boots on;
John had a
Great Big
Waterproof
Hat;
John had a
Great Big
Waterproof
Macintosh –
And that
(Said John)
Is
That.

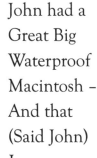

King John's Christmas

King John was not a good man –
    He had his little ways.
And sometimes no one spoke to him
    For days and days and days.
And men who came across him,
    When walking in the town,
Gave him a supercilious stare,
Or passed with noses in the air –
And bad King John stood dumbly there,
    Blushing beneath his crown.

King John was not a good man,
    And no good friends had he.
He stayed in every afternoon...
    But no one came to tea.
And, round about December,
    The cards upon his shelf
Which wished him lots of Christmas cheer,
And fortune in the coming year,
Were never from his near and dear,
    But only from himself.

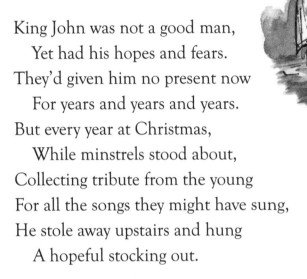

King John was not a good man,
   Yet had his hopes and fears.
They'd given him no present now
   For years and years and years.
But every year at Christmas,
   While minstrels stood about,
Collecting tribute from the young
For all the songs they might have sung,
He stole away upstairs and hung
   A hopeful stocking out.

King John was not a good man,
   He lived his life aloof;
Alone he thought a message out
   While climbing up the roof.
He wrote it down and propped it
   Against the chimney stack:
"TO ALL AND SUNDRY – NEAR AND FAR –
F. CHRISTMAS IN PARTICULAR."
And signed it not "Johannes R."
   But very humbly, "JACK."

"I want some crackers,
    And I want some candy;
I think a box of chocolates
    Would come in handy;
I don't mind oranges,
    I do like nuts!
And I SHOULD like a pocket-knife
    That really cuts.
And, oh! Father Christmas, if you love
    me at all,
Bring me a big, red india-rubber ball!"

King John was not a good man –
    He wrote this message out,
And gat him to his room again,
    Descending by the spout.
And all that night he lay there,
    A prey to hopes and fears.
"I think that's him a-coming now,"
    (Anxiety bedewed his brow.)
"He'll bring one present, anyhow –
    The first I've had for years."

"Forget about the crackers,
    And forget about the candy;
I'm sure a box of chocolates
    Would never come in handy;
I don't like oranges,
    I don't want nuts,
And I HAVE got a pocket-knife
    That almost cuts.
But, oh! Father Christmas, if you love me at all,
Bring me a big, red india-rubber ball!"

King John was not a good man –
    Next morning when the sun
Rose up to tell a waiting world
    That Christmas had begun,
And people seized their stockings,
    And opened them with glee,
And crackers, toys and games appeared,
And lips with sticky sweets were smeared,
King John said grimly: "As I feared,
    Nothing again for me!"

"I did want crackers,
    And I did want candy;
I know a box of chocolates
    Would come in handy;
I do love oranges,
    I did want nuts.
I haven't got a pocket-knife –
    Not one that cuts.
And, oh! if Father Christmas had loved me at all,
He would have brought a big, red india-rubber ball!"

King John stood by the window,
    And frowned to see below
The happy bands of boys and girls
    All playing in the snow.
A while he stood there watching,
    And envying them all…
When through the window big and red
There hurtled by his royal head,
And bounced and fell upon the bed,
    An india-rubber ball!

AND OH, FATHER CHRISTMAS,
    MY BLESSINGS ON YOU FALL
        FOR BRINGING HIM
        A BIG, RED
        INDIA-RUBBER
        BALL!

In the Dark

I've had my supper,
  And *had* my supper,
    And HAD my supper and all;
I've heard the story
  Of Cinderella,
    And how she went to the ball;
I've cleaned my teeth,
  And I've said my prayers,
    And I've cleaned and said them right;
And they've all of them been
  And kissed me lots,
    They've all of them said, "Good-night."

So – here I am in the dark alone,
  There's nobody here to see;

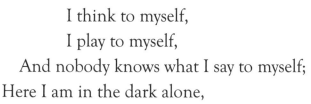

I think to myself,
I play to myself,
And nobody knows what I say to myself;
Here I am in the dark alone,
What is it going to be?
I can think whatever I like to think,
I can play whatever I like to play,
I can laugh whatever I like to laugh,
There's nobody here but me.
I'm talking to a rabbit...

I'm talking to the sun...
I think I am a hundred –
I'm one.
I'm lying in a forest...
I'm lying in a cave...
I'm talking to a Dragon...
I'm BRAVE.
I'm lying on my left side...
I'm lying on my right...
I'll play a lot tomorrow...
. . . .
I'll think a lot tomorrow...
. . . .
I'll laugh...
a lot...
tomorrow...
(Heigh-ho!)

Good-night.

About the Author

*A.A.Milne with his son
Christopher Robin,
and Winnie-the-Pooh*

A.A.Milne was born in London in 1882. He began his writing career with humorous pieces for *Punch* magazine. It was in this publication, in 1923, that Winnie-the-Pooh made his first appearance in the poem 'Teddy Bear'. Milne also wrote plays and by the time *When We Were Very Young*, his first book of poems for children, was published in 1924, he had already made his name as a dramatist and novelist.

About the Illustrator

E.H.Shepard was born in 1879, became known as the 'Man who drew Pooh', but was also an acclaimed artist in his own right. Shepard won a scholarship to the Royal Academy of Arts, and later, like Milne, worked for *Punch* magazine as a cartoonist and an illustrator. Shepard's illustrations of Winnie~the~Pooh and the friends of the Hundred Acre Wood have become classics in their own right and are recognised all over the world.

Ernest Howard Shepard, "the man who drew Pooh".

Shepard wrote: 'It was a happy task for me making these drawings and I have grown to love the little folk of these stories.' He often adapted or revisited the original illustrations, such as this iconic one from The House at Pooh Corner, *which he made into a Christmas card.*